Scottish Hauntings

Born into a Lanarkshire police family in 1913, Donald Grant Campbell served for over thirty years in the Perth and Kinross Constabulary and thereafter in the Civil Service.

A life-long interest in the history of Scotland, and in particular that part in the heart of the Grampians which is now being turned into the vast playground of the ski world, has led him to collect legendary tales both verbal and written.

In this book the tales have been collected from real happenings, from fiction, old books and newspapers, and also from historical and modern sources stretching from the wild sea-tossed rocks of the Flannan Isles to Galloway in the south.

Not all happenings can be explained: the author was born on 9 April; his father, daughter and a grandson were all born on the same day and month.

Also by Grant Campbell in Piccolo

Scottish Fairy Tales

Grant Campbell

Scottish Hauntings

Illustrated by Jane Bottomley

A Piccolo Original
Piccolo Books

First published 1982 by Pan Books Ltd,
Cavaye Place, London SW10 9PG
10 9 8 7 6 5 4 3
© Grant Campbell 1982
Illustrations © Jane Bottomley 1982
ISBN 0 330 26618 7
Printed and bound in Great Britain by
Hazell Watson & Viney Limited,
Member of the BPCC Group,
Aylesbury, Bucks

This book is sold subject to the condition that it
shall not, by way of trade or otherwise, be lent, re-sold,
hired out or otherwise circulated without the publisher's prior
consent in any form of binding or cover other than that in which
it is published and without a similar condition including this
condition being imposed on the subsequent purchaser

To my grandchildren
Neil and Lynne

Contents

The Sites of Scottish Hauntings

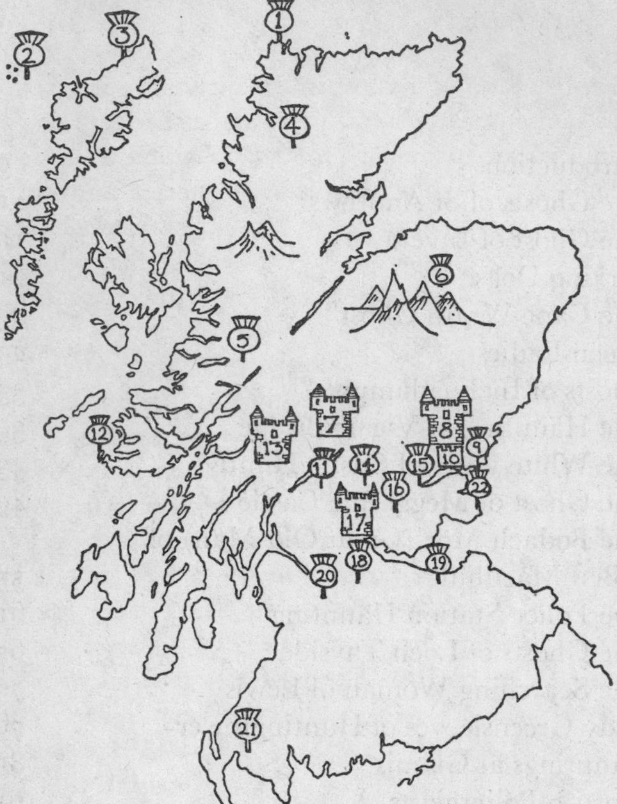

Key

1 Cape Wrath	9 Dundee	16 Kinross
2 Flannan Isles	10 Castle Huntly	17 Stirling
3 Lewis	11 Loch Tay	18 Avonbridge
4 Inchnadamph	12 Iona and Mull	19 Edinburgh
5 Loch Morar	13 Inverawe	20 Glasgow
6 Aviemore	14 Crieff	21 Glenluce
7 Glenlyon	15 Perth	22 St Andrews
8 Glamis		

Introduction

The definition of a ghost in the dictionary is given as 'the soul of man, a spirit appearing after death or pertaining to an apparition'. Such a definition seems sceptical but the many thousands of stories and corroborated reports prove that a number of factors have to be considered – especially in the present day, when we find ourselves in the realms of space, the paranormal and unidentified flying objects (UFOs).

Many people are reluctant to supply information on a subject which is often linked to a past tragedy or crisis in their lives. The shut-off mechanism in the brain of an elderly person is well known: past or forgotten incidents seem to become very clear in the mind, while the memories of recent happenings disappear.

I remember one instance of an elderly lady living alone who maintained that, while sitting in her lounge, she saw small doll-like figures in pixie dress walk along the top of her piano and then disappear. I sat with her on one occasion when she claimed that the dolls were present on the piano top. I saw no dolls and experienced nothing unusual but I was inclined to think that the dolls might have some connection with the old lady's childhood, which had been spent in that same large house. I asked her if she could remember any of the old tunes which she might have played on the piano as a young girl. With some hesitation she went forward to the keyboard and started to play – explaining that she had not played for years. After a few minutes she stopped playing and in some surprise informed me that the pixie dolls were no longer walking on top of the piano. She also said that she now remembered that her younger sister played with pixie-dressed dolls on top of the piano. Needless to say, the old lady never again reported seeing the dolls on the piano top.

People who have seen or experienced ghosts or ghostly manifestations give some indication that there is a vast area of knowledge yet to be explored. The great number of people who have *not* seen a ghost or experienced strange happenings do not add up to a sceptical majority as many people believe.

It is estimated that one in eight people will see a ghost at some time during their lives and also that two out of every three such 'ghost witnesses' will be women. In the distant past, hauntings in Scotland which were seen and reported were put down to witchcraft, and many people suffered death by burning and other cruel means. It is a long time since Scotland had a witchcraft trial but the same cannot be said for England when in 1944 a Scotswoman named Helen Duncan was convicted of contravening the Witchcraft Act of 1735 in the war-damaged Old Bailey and sentenced to a term of imprisonment.

Despite the flow of oil and tourism the Highlands of Scotland still produce exceptional ghost tales of a modern character. In spite of the fact that Scotland lost most of her definite Celtic character when the Gaelic language was chased from the Church and Courts of Law, the Highland ghost still displays its own peculiar parochial tendencies. The real question is: have you seen a ghost? Many have; but, if not, that pleasure is still to come.

Grant Campbell
Perth, 1981

The Ghosts of St Andrews

In that part of Scotland known as the Kingdom of Fife stands the ancient university town of St Andrews, on the sea coast midway between the firths of Tay and Forth. The most venerable ghost in the town is that of the monk who murdered Prior Robert.

The Prior of St Andrews, Robert de Montrose, had precedence over all the other priors and abbots of Scotland in the days of King Robert III. It happened that a certain monk by the name of Thomas Plater was jealous of the good Prior Robert, who ruled the priory with a firm hand. Plater managed to obtain possession of a dirk, which he concealed within his robe, and resolved to put the good prior to death.

It was well known that each evening after vespers Prior Robert walked in a certain direction through the darkened cloisters to his dormitory. One night, as he was about to climb the stairs to his sleeping quarters, the Monk Plater leapt out of the shadows where he had been hiding and stabbed the good Prior. But the hurried stabbing did not prove to be immediately fatal and the victim lingered on in pain for three days. Before he died he managed to reveal the identity of his attacker. Plater was tried and found guilty of murder. He was sentenced to solitary confinement in a cell for life but did not live very long after being sentenced. His ghost was doomed to haunt the cathedral and its grounds in the coming centuries.

The ghost of Plater was said to appear when the priory bell was sounded to call the brethren to vespers. One reported sighting was of the evil-looking face of a monk looking out from one of the windows in one of the cathedral towers.

At one time, when part of the priory was being restored, a number of human bones were discovered and reburied. The story is also told of how the apparition of a monk dressed in a long robe appeared beside the bed of a local hotel worker and conveyed the message that he was the ghost of Thomas Plater and the masons working in the priory buildings had disturbed his remains. The apparition continued to appear at intervals, and arrangements were made for the skeletons which had been found to be exhumed and buried in consecrated ground.

In one of the vaults of the priory an altar was erected and an appropriate service held. The service was conducted by a Benedictine monk and the local priest in July 1898, over five hundred years after the murder. However, in recent years the ghost of a monk has been seen again in St Andrews and it is possible that the bones of the murderer still remain in unconsecrated ground.

*

Some years ago one of the St Andrews university professors, who lived in an old house in the vicinity of the Pends, asked one of the lecturers to spend the Sunday evening with him at his home. Time went by in conversation until it was nearly 1 AM on the Monday morning when the lecturer said 'Good night' to his friend and started on his way to his own lodgings.

It was a clear moonlit night and North Street, St Andrews, appeared deserted, when suddenly the lecturer saw a man coming towards him down the street. The approaching man had a stern look on his face and was dressed in a long gown with clerical markings. His long dark beard was streaked with grey. Behind the gowned figure marched another man who appeared to be some sort of soldier, wearing a steel helmet of a very old pattern. There was no sound of footfalls but as the clerical gentleman passed close by he fixed the lecturer with a strange look. No sound was uttered.

The lecturer, who was acquainted with old paintings and costume descriptions, was suddenly aware that he had seen the ghost of John Knox, the well-known historical figure of the Scottish Reformation. The man hurried back to the home of the professor and told him of what he had seen. The appearance of the 'soldier' remained a puzzle until it was discovered through local research that, while Knox was in St Andrews, he was escorted for his own protection by a member of the Town Guard.

The Ghost of Inverawe

Between Loch Awe and Loch Etive, in the shadow of high Ben Cruachan, amidst the wild and picturesque scenery of the Western Highlands of Scotland, stood the ancient house of Inverawe. As was the custom before the middle of the last century – and to this day in parts of the Highlands – no door was ever locked. Visitors in peace were made welcome and given shelter at the fireside.

Late one night, the Laird of Inverawe, Duncan Campbell, was sitting alone in the old hall when there was a loud knocking at the door. Before Duncan could rise to find the cause a stranger staggered into the hall.

The stranger flung himself at the feet of the Laird who saw that the stranger's clothing was smeared with blood. The Laird was unable to distinguish the tartan of the kilt worn by the man, as the garment was faded and torn. The man was gasping for breath and just managed to beg for shelter, saying that he was being chased by friends of a man he had killed in a fair fight. On his knees the man continued to appeal and explained that his pursuers were not far behind in the Pass of Brander.

Taking pity on the stranger the Laird said that he would give him shelter, and took him to a safe cellar in the house. 'Swear on your dirk that you will shelter me,' said the man. Duncan Campbell then swore as promised before leaving the man in the safe hiding place.

Within a few minutes of his returning to the hall two armed men arrived at the house. The two men were related to Duncan and they told him that his foster brother had been murdered and that they, along with other members of the clan, had been in close pursuit of the murderer, who had disappeared in the vicinity of Inverawe. Duncan was heartbroken at the news of the death but the oath giving protection under the old clan law could not be broken for three clear days even for a blood feud. He told the men that he had no knowledge of the fugitive and they went away after searching the grounds.

In great distress the Laird lay down to rest in his dark bedchamber and was soon asleep. Waking suddenly in terror from the events of the night, he was aware of the moonlight in the room, which appeared to silhouette the figure of the murdered foster brother standing by his bed. He then heard a voice crying, 'Inverawe, Inverawe, blood has been shed. Shield not the murderer.'

In the morning the Laird went to the hiding place and told the stranger that he could no longer harbour him as he suspected that he was responsible for the murder of his foster brother. 'Duncan Campbell, Laird of Inverawe!' replied the man, 'you have sworn to protect me.' Duncan was torn between his duty to the family of the murdered man and his sworn oath. He promised not to betray the stranger but told him that it was impossible to keep him hidden in the house at Inverawe. That night Duncan led the man to a cave on the mountainside and left him with food for two days.

Returning to his house, he lay half asleep and tired with grief, thinking of the strange coincidence which had caused him to give sanctuary to the murderer of his own foster brother. Could the ancient loyalties be broken and revenge exacted? From the darkness he again heard a voice which reminded him of the dead foster brother crying, 'Inverawe, Inverawe, blood has been shed. Shield not the murderer.'

At daybreak Duncan made his way to the cave with still the thought of revenge in his mind. Arriving at the cave he found that the man had gone, taking away all evidence that the cave had been occupied. Later that day he attended the funeral of his foster brother and he learned that the murderer had not been traced.

When Duncan retired to bed on the third night he fell

fast asleep from the exhaustion of the day, but in the early hours he was awakened by the sound of rushing wind as if a storm had hit the house. He then saw by his bedside the form of his dead foster brother standing naked in a grey light which seemed to show up the bloodstained throat. Duncan sat up and tried to explain what he had done but the ghostly form became menacing and said, 'Farewell, farewell, Inverawe, till we meet at TICONDEROGA!' The form then vanished through the wall of the room.

The ghostly figure did not appear again in the house of Inverawe. Duncan always remembered the name TICONDEROGA but he had no knowledge of such a place. He never mentioned it to his family and the word remained a puzzle to him.

Some time later, Duncan joined the 42nd Highland Regiment, known as the Black Watch, which was mostly officered by members of the Clan Campbell. The regiment was raised to keep the peace in the Highlands of Scotland. He rose to the rank of Major and accompanied the regiment when it was sent to America to fight against the French under Montcalm in 1758.

Now far away from Inverawe with the Black Watch – in which his son also served as a junior officer – Duncan sat at a camp fire thinking of home while at the same time making plans for an attack on the French-held Fort Carillion at Crown Point where the waters of Lake George and Lake Champlain meet. The attack was planned for early the next morning and a number of Indian guides were standing about near the camp-fire. To his surprise, Duncan heard one of the guides speak the word TICONDEROGA and to his horror he learned that this was the Indian name for Fort Carillion.

He then told his son and fellow-officers the story of the murder of his foster brother and the words spoken by the ghost which appeared after he had given sanctuary to the murderer. He also told them that he would be killed during the attack on the fort.

The attack on the fort started at daybreak; and, as with many of the mistakes made by the British in the course of that campaign, the defenders were not the lightly armed inexperienced troops which had been expected. Grape-shot and bits of iron scrap tore into the attacking British force. The redcoat waves were broken and few managed to climb the palisades.

The final assault was to be that of the tartan-clad Highlanders and, as the battle pipes set their blood

afire, Duncan led his men forward. He climbed the last stockade successfully and remnants of his men assembled about him to finish the attack. As he gave the order to storm the fort buildings the Laird of Inverawe was hit by a stray bullet. He fell back into the arms of his son.

Duncan Campbell died as a result of the wound and with his last breath he mumbled, 'TICONDEROGA, peace at last.'

Barking Dogs

Loch Morar in Inverness-shire is the deepest stretch of water in Britain, measuring 1,045 feet at its deepest point. A monster with a long neck, large head and a body with several humps (much the same description as that of the Loch Ness monster)has been seen breaking the surface of the water. In addition to the monster in the loch there are also the 'Barking dogs of Morar', a well-known legend in the district.

It is said that a man named MacDonald left his cottage at the head of Loch Morar to seek his fortune in Canada. He was forced to leave his favourite black bitch in the care of a friend as he set out on his long journey. The bitch was due to have pups and she started to pine away after her master left. She did not take kindly to her new abode and one day she managed to escape. She dived into Loch Morar and swam across to a little island where her pups were later born. There was plenty of food on the island in the form of rabbits and wild fowl, and in time the pups grew up to be great savage dogs and would not allow any person to land on the island.

About four years later the owner of the bitch returned from Canada, only to be told by his friend that the bitch had escaped and gone to live on the island with her offspring. Anxious to see his old bitch again, the man asked his friend to take him over to the island in his small rowing boat. The friend warned him of the danger from the wild dogs; despite the warning, the owner of the bitch insisted that he would be safe. He was then rowed over to the island. His friend waited beside the small rowing boat on the shore.

When the bitch saw her old master she ran to him and started to make a great fuss of him. The other dogs of the pack became jealous of the affection their mother showed for this man. All at once they sprang upon him and tore him to pieces. The friend saw from the shore what had happened and made his way back to the mainland to tell of the tragedy.

Ever since then, many local people and visitors to the district have heard phantom dogs barking around the disused cottage near the head of Loch Morar.

*

Another tale of the barking and yelping of a phantom dog comes from the Blairgowrie district of Perthshire; but so far as can be ascertained no living person has seen or heard this ghost dog of Mause.

According to local legend a man named William Soutar was the farmer at Middle Mause. Some time in mid December 1728 he and his servants were working in the fields when they heard the yelping and barking of a dog which appeared to be in distress. At nightfall they saw a large, dark grey coloured dog, but due to falling darkness it could not further be identified.

Soutar continued to see the dog on subsequent nights during the winter and it seemed to come nearer to him each time. One night, when he was going home over the bridge across the Lornty burn which runs into the

river Isla, the dog appeared again. But this time, in addition to the bark, Soutar heard the words, '*Within eight days, do or die.*'

William Soutar was very upset and he told his brother about the meeting with the dog at the bridge. The next night his brother James accompanied him to the same spot and in due course the dog came forward, whining, and stopped about ten yards from the two men. It is said that the dog then directed the two men to a nearby spot where a man and his dog had been murdered and buried. The local minister and the lairds who owned the ground were informed by the brothers and a search was made. The bones were found and given a Christian burial in the old churchyard at the Hill o'Blair.

One other recorded version of this tale is that the Laird of Rochalle had a quarrel with the local minister over the refusal to baptize a child born to one of the Laird's servants. William Soutar was the chief elder of the kirk and the Laird believed that he was responsible for the action of the minister. The Laird then arranged that his butler be dressed up in sheep skins and appear to William Soutar near the bridge over the Lornty. The trick worked so well that the Laird arranged for an old human skull and other animal bones to be placed in a hiding place as described by the alleged phantom dog.

If the phantom dog of Mause was a hoax it would account for the fact that there is no evidence of the dog having been seen or heard since the time of the Soutar brothers.

The Cape Wrath Ghost

In the extreme north-east of Sutherland the angry sea has created many beautiful bays, including the one known as Sandwood Bay about five miles south of Cape Wrath. It is said to be the haunting ground of a ghostly seaman. Sandwood Bay is a very bleak spot in winter, and driftwood and wreckage are often found after winter gales. Both summer visitors and local crofters collecting driftwood have told of the strange apparition described as a tall seaman wearing sea boots, cap and a dark jacket with brass buttons.

Some locals have been so frightened by the appearance of the ghostly figure that they have dropped their bundles of driftwood and run from the scene. Others, of a stronger heart, have tried to make contact but when they move forward towards the figure, it suddenly disappears leaving no trace of any footprints in the sand.

Throughout the years the remains of many drowned seaman have been found in this particular bay. Local legend has it that the figure seen is one of the drowned men.

A partly ruined cottage stands nearby, and people seeking shelter within its walls have heard the sound of ghostly footsteps. In one instance it is claimed that a bearded face wearing a sailor's cap was seen looking in at one of the windows. English visitors who stayed in the cottage overnight also heard the sound of heavy footsteps inside the building.

In Scotland many ruins can be found where once a thriving community existed and also in lonely places where disused shepherds' cottages are now used as mountain shelters. Such places are associated with the bloodstained history of long ago and even with the modern tragedies of mountaineering and hill-walking – strange sounds and shadows cannot always be explained away.

Green Ladies

Throughout history the colour green has been considered unlucky in Scotland. It was said that green was the colour used by the fairies, who were supposed to take offence if mortal men and women presumed to wear it.

After the battle of Flodden, a heavy defeat by the English with great loss of life, many of the clansmen were dressed in green tartan. This may also be responsible for the superstition.

The colour has also been associated with spectres or ghosts haunting many old Scottish castles and mansion houses. In most cases the spectre has been that of a young or beautiful lady dressed in green robes.

Very often the appearance of a Green Lady was a sign of calamity to a noble house or to a particular individual. There have been many exceptions to this general rule but up to the present day the superstition is still very strong. On the other hand, green is a popular colour in France and was much in favour with the ancient Druids.

In the Blairgowrie district of Perthshire there grew a legend of a beautiful lady dressed in green who haunted Ardblair Castle, the home of the Blair Oliphant family. She was also seen at Newton Castle, the home of the Macpherson family.

About the time of Robert the Bruce, according to

legend, the Blair family and their neighbours the Drummonds who then occupied Newton Castle had some differences of opinion which caused bitter feuding. The feuding of the elders was probably over some question of land ownership and did not appear to extend to the younger members of the two families.

One of the younger members of the Blair family fell in love with Lady Jean Drummond of Newton and a secret marriage took place. Immediately after the marriage Lady Jean mysteriously disappeared. The story was put about that she had been taken away by Water Kelpies because she had been wearing a green dress on the day of her marriage, which put her in their power. The more probable explanation for the disappearance was that her secret had been discovered and she drown-

ed herself or was murdered and her body hidden in the marshland.

The ghost of the young lady dressed in green has been seen on summer afternoons sitting on a window seat in the long gallery at Ardblair. She never frightens anyone, and either sits at a window or passes through the corridors and into other rooms without making a sound. A ghost of the same description is said to haunt the grounds of Newton Castle.

It is said that in 1939 the Green Lady was the cause of evacuees from Glasgow leaving their billets in the tower and long gallery at Ardblair.

*

It is also recorded that members of a family living in the Blairgowrie district claim to have seen a young woman dressed in in a green cape and hood standing by the side of the stream leading to the West Mill of Rattray. Her clothing appeared to be dripping and the apparition seemed to float away in the darkness of the night. Those who saw the apparition put it down to the ghost of a woman who had been found drowned in the water rushing under the mill.

*

Another local ghost is the Green Lady of Castle Wemyss in Fife, who wanders through the corridors of the castle wearing a trailing gown of green silk. It is said that a rustling noise is often heard as if from the trailing gown. It is now many years since the Green Lady was last seen and no information has been obtained as to why she appeared and then disappeared, but her story may be known to the family.

*

Another Green Lady is the ghost of Fyvie Castle in Aberdeenshire, who is said to emerge from a secret room known as the 'haunted chamber' and glide noiselessly through other rooms and corridors. The apparition always seems to glide above the floor rather than walk and disappears through doors and solid walls.

*

The castle of Stirling built on the site of a Roman signal station commands a view of the river Forth and the surrounding countryside including the historic battlefield of Bannockburn. Stirling surpassed Edinburgh in strategic importance, and for 500 years the Kings of Scotland resided in the castle. Like Edinburgh, the old town spills down from the castle rock; one can imagine the clatter of horses mingling with the marching of armoured men. Little wonder that this old castle is associated with many strange happenings, which include the appearance of a Green Lady. It is believed that the appearance of this ghostly figure is a warning of disaster.

In the past, serious fires have broken out after a reported sighting. Some say that the original Green Lady was a maidservant to Mary, Queen of Scots, who rescued the Queen from her four-poster bed, the draperies of which had caught fire while the Queen was asleep.

It has also been claimed that the Green Lady was the daughter of a governor of the castle who was in love with an officer of the garrison. The officer was accidentally killed by the governor, and the girl, on learning of the accident, was so distressed that she threw herself to her death from the castle battlements. Quite apart from the army cook who fainted in one of the mess kitchens when he discovered the Green Lady standing at his elbow, the castle has been the scene of many strange happenings within recent years.

The large section in the upper square of the castle is known as the 'Governor's block' and it is in this part that recent hauntings have been reported. The Governor's block has a room at the top of a flight of stairs where footsteps are heard going across the ceiling although there is no room or passage of any description situated above.

From time to time the room in question was occupied by officers of the Argyll and Sutherland Highlanders while it was the headquarters of the regiment. The officers occupying the room were mostly men who had

fought during the Second World War, and were not easily frightened, but they were often disturbed by the distinct sound of footsteps. It is recorded in the regimental history that in the 1820s there was a sentry beat along a battlement which existed at that time above the Governor's block. One night a relief sentry taking over guard duty found the previous guardsman lying at his post with a look of horror on his dead face.

Ghosts of Inchnadamph

The small hamlet of Inchnadamph at the head of Loch Assynt in Sutherland consists of a church, a shooting lodge, a hotel and a few cottages where legends abound. Nearby, in the direction of Lochinver, can be seen the ruins of Ardvreck Castle, which is situated on a small peninsula in Loch Assynt. It was once the stronghold of the MacLeods of Assynt where James Graham, Marquis of Montrose, was imprisoned after his betrayal by one of the MacLeods. Local folk maintain that the ghost of Montrose still haunts the ruins.

The other ruin in the district is Invercalda House, which takes its name from the Calda burn beside which it stands. The house was built by the Mackenzies, who inherited Assynt in the seventeenth century. It was burnt to the ground with all its inhabitants, except one piper, early on a Sunday morning only two weeks after it was occupied.

The legend says that the Mackenzies had arranged a family gathering, and their merry-making carried on well into the Sabbath morning. The official piper much against his will was forced to play on after the midnight hour. Assynt people believe to this day that the fire was a manifestation of Divine wrath for the breaking of the Sabbath, and that the piper was allowed to escape the flames because his intentions had been good.

The remains of those who perished in the fire still lie

in the crumbling family vault in Inchnadamph churchyard. In recent years the ghost of a woman has been seen on the road near the Invercalda ruins. One can look through the vault entrance in the churchyard, but don't dare go inside! Water drips from the roof even in good weather. It is said that anybody hit by the drip of water will be dead within a year.

A number of local people have experienced strange happenings and they will tell you that Inchnadamph ghosts are not just imagination. Some years ago near the former shooting lodge known as Stronchrubie House the local schoolteacher was cycling along the public road on a winter evening when she saw a fearsome black dog. The dog seemed to disappear across the road with a silent wolf-like stride. In this same house two local girls were disturbed by a loud noise as if dishes were being smashed in the kitchen. On investigation they didn't find a single dish out of place. Unexplained bell ringing has also been heard.

*

Supernatural occurences in this part of Sutherland appear to keep up to date with the modern world – on numerous occasions the headlights of ghostly motorcars have appeared. One such recorded incident was on the lonely road from Lochinver which runs alongside Loch Assynt. The driver of a car suddenly became aware of powerful headlights approaching over the brow of a hill, but on reaching the top of the hill the lights had disappeared and she saw no sign of any other vehicle.

Another case was that of two friends walking together on the same road by the side of the loch when they saw what they took to be the dipped headlights of a car stopped in a roadside layby and facing them. As the two men came near to the layby the lights suddenly disappeared, leaving no trace of a car or any other vehicle.

*

Some years ago a young shepherd who lived by himself in a lonely cottage some distance from Inchnadamph was found drowned in the shallow pool of a burn near the foot of the mountain known as Ben More. He had apparently fallen and hit his head on a stone and been knocked unconscious into the burn. A few evenings before, he had been sitting in the hotel kitchen at Inchnadamph. He did not appear to be his usual cheery self and on being asked what was wrong stated that he had had a bad dream and could not get it out of his head. He dreamed that he had seen his own dead body lying out on the heather by the side of Ben More.

The Haunting at Vicars Bridge

Late on a dark December evening in the year 1865, Alexander McEwan, a baker's vanman, drove his horse-van across the old stone bridge spanning the river Devon and started up the hill towards Blairingone village in the county of Kinross.

The van later arrived at a customer's door at Blairingone without the driver. The alarm was raised and some of the villagers started out to search for the missing man.

They had not travelled far in their search when they found the missing vanman lying by the roadside riddled with shotgun pellets. He was still alive but unable to speak and died in a house to which he was carried by the search party.

The roadside from Vicars Bridge was bounded by a thick wood and was a favourite place for poachers shooting pheasants. It was clear that murder had been done.

It was also estimated that the sum of more than £5 was missing from the vanman's cash bag. A further search in daylight revealed a shotgun which had been hidden under the arch of the bridge.

A young man, Joseph Bell, a well-known poacher, was arrested for the murder. He was found guilty at his trial in Perth and was subsequently hanged in that city on 22 May 1866. Despite the evidence and the

unanimous verdict of the jury, Bell claimed to the day of his execution that he was innocent of the crime.

However, since the public execution of Bell it is said that the clipclop of horses' hoofs can be heard at times passing over the old bridge. Some maintain that the sound is made by small boulders in the river-bed being moved by the current.

Two local farmers claim that a figure of a man dressed in old-fashioned clothing was seen in the headlights of their car one winter night. The figure seemed to come from the wood and then disappeared instantly from the centre of the road.

The two farmers were returning from the annual dinner of the Kinross Jolly Beggars Burns Club. Having been entertained with the tale of Tam O' Shanter, the thought of warlocks and witches may have aroused their imagination.

*

On another occasion a young farmer and his girlfriend were on their way home in a small pick-up truck from a dance in Kinross. While the vehicle was crossing Vicars Bridge they both heard a strange noise. Having heard stories of the murder and the ghost at the bridge, the young man did not stop to investigate.

On reaching his destination with the girl still in a state of fright he discovered an unwelcome passenger in the back of the truck. As the young man stepped out of the truck he saw a tramp-like figure trying to climb over the high sides of the truck. The tramp, who was under the influence of drink, had managed to climb aboard while the truck was parked in Kinross, and had fallen asleep on bunches of straw carried on the back of the truck. The man had awakened from his drunken sleep near to Vicars Bridge and the noise heard was the unwanted passenger banging on the wooden sides.

Despite the many probable explanations, some locals still maintain that on a night when the narrow road leading from the bridge is bathed in moonlight a strange figure can be seen standing near a tree opposite where the vanman had been shot and robbed. The figure is also said to have been seen floating over the parapet of the bridge into the water.

The White Lady of Castle Huntly

The fifteenth-century residence known as Castle Huntly, which became a Borstal institution in 1947, is situated seven miles west of Dundee in the Carse of Gowrie. Baron Gray of Fowlis was granted a licence by King James II allowing him to build the castle.

The castle is now surrounded by fertile farmland but it was built on one of the few locations in the district where the solid rock is near to the surface; the landscape in ancient times was marshy wilderness. The building at its highest point is 116 feet from ground level with walls ten to fourteen feet thick.

The castle and estate came in 1614 into the possession of the Lyon family of Glamis, bought by the Earl of Strathmore, who changed the name to Castle Lyon. The 7th Earl of Strathmore married Miss Elizabeth Bowes of Streatham in 1767 and assumed the name Bowes-Lyon. He died in 1776 and his widow, Countess Bowes-Lyon, returned to stay in London. The estate was then sold to George Paterson of Dundee who amassed a great fortune with the East India Company. His wife was a direct descendant of the original owners, and he changed the name back to Castle Huntly.

The Paterson family spent a great deal of money on the property and also added the Georgian portion on the north-east side together with a new roof and central tower. The last Paterson to occupy the castle was

Colonel Adrian Gordon Paterson who died on 5 June 1940, three years after succeeding. In 1946 his widow sold the castle to the government. The Patersons' only son had been drowned as a boy in a yachting accident on the Tay.

The legend of the White Lady of Castle Huntly which originated in an actual tragedy is not disputed. While the Lyon family occupied the castle it is said that a daughter of the house became the lover of a manservant. When her parents learned of their love, the daughter was banished to a bedroom high up on the tower looking out on to the battlements. What happened to the manservant is not recorded but it is a good guess that he was thrown alive into the vaulted dungeon of the castle, which is still a gruesome place.

The poor young girl must have suffered agony and hardship being banished and locked up in the high tower bedroom. The story, which has been passed from one generation to another, is that the young prisoner found relief by throwing herself from her prison window, and was killed. It has also been suggested that she was pushed out of the window to her death.

Over the years, residents of the Carse of Gowrie have claimed to have seen the White Lady ghost in the vicinity of the castle dressed in long white flowing robes. One appearance was recorded at the end of the last century by one of the Castle Huntly lairds. Since then strange sounds have been heard within the castle, and one man reported that he had seen the White Lady moving between certain trees within the grounds.

The castle is now used as the administration block for the institution, but after being taken over by the govern-

ment and prior to dormitory quarters and workshops being built within the grounds over a period of years the castle was fully occupied. One bedroom which looks on to the battlements at the top of the castle was occupied by inmates who worked in the cookhouse.

From this bedroom high in the castle one boy reported to the Matron that he had been awakened by something. He then saw a figure which he took to be a boy or man at the foot of his bed. The figure seemed to float away and disappear into a cupboard in the room. He said that the figure was bareheaded and was dressed in a double-breasted jacket in the fashion of the 1930s. The Matron paid no attention to the story and suggested to the boy that he had been dreaming.

The boy completed his training and left the establishment. The room continued to be used as a bedroom by the boys employed in the cookhouse. No further reports were received by the Matron about strange happenings in the room and she never mentioned the matter to any other inmate or member of staff.

Eight years went by and, as expected, a complete change-over of inmates had taken place. The Matron was then surprised one morning when a boy from the same bedroom reported that he had seen a ghost at the foot of his bed which seemed to disappear into the same cupboard as reported eight years before. The only description the boy could give was that the figure he had seen was wearing a funny double-breasted jacket.

As already stated the only son and heir to the last private owner, Colonel Adrian Gordon Paterson, was drowned in a yachting accident on the Tay. In the graveyard at Longforgan parish church there is a family gravestone and following that of Colonel Paterson himself the inscription reads:

His only son Richard David Charles 1930–1939

Could the drowned boy have been wearing a double-breasted jacket at the time of his death and taken over the haunting from the White Lady?

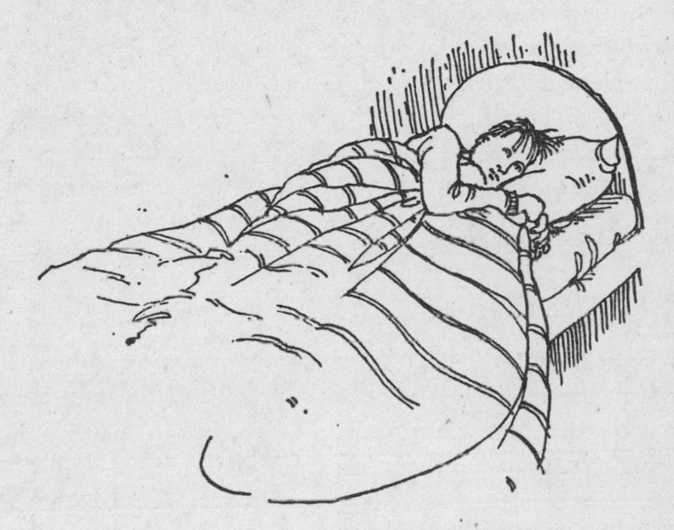

The Ghost of Meggernie Castle

In the heart of historic Perthshire lies Glenlyon, which is rich in legends of fairies and goblins as well as stories of ghosts and people with second sight.

As you enter the Pass of Glenlyon from the village of Fortingall, Britain's oldest living tree, the Fortingall Yew, is to be found by the side of the churchyard wall where it is known to have stood for well over 1,500 years. The river Lyon leaps over the crags through a deep gorge on its way to join the river Tay. The mountains rise straight from the banks of the river, which flows from Loch Lyon at the head of the glen, and at many places stand remaining parts of the primeval Caledonian forest.

About halfway up the glen near the Bridge of Balgie a long avenue runs through an archway along the bank of the Lyon leading to Meggernie Castle, the oldest part of which was built about 1585. Later additions were made to the castle by Captain Campbell, who was in charge of the troops carrying out the massacre of Glencoe in 1692.

With complete disregard for historical fact it is said that inhabitants of Glenlyon were led by their chief, Captain Campbell, to carry out the massacre of the MacDonalds of Glencoe. In fact, Captain Campbell was an officer in His Majesty's army and was sent with a detachment of regular soldiers from the Argylls regiment; they enjoyed the hospitality of the MacDonalds for a fortnight prior to Captain Campbell's receiving the dispatch which gave him instructions to carry out the massacre. He was also warned that the instructions were to be carried out without fond or favour – else he might expect to be dealt with as one not true to King or government, nor a man fit to carry commissions in the King's service.

The haunting of Meggernie Castle is attributed to the time when the castle was owned by the Chief of the Clan Menzies, who was very jealous of his young and beautiful wife. In a fit of madness he murdered his young wife in the tower of the castle.

Menzies then concealed the body in a chest and

placed the chest in a closet between two rooms in the tower. After locking the tower and making sure no one would enter, he left the castle at night and did not return for some time.

On his return, Menzies spread the story that he had been travelling on the Continent with his young wife and that she had been accidentally and tragically drowned. The story about the death of his wife by drowning was believed by the local people; Menzies then decided to dispose of the remains in the nearby graveyard in the castle park.

According to legend he cut the body in two and crept down to the graveyard in the dead of night where he managed to bury the lower half. The identifiable part of the body was left in the closet. The following morning Menzies was found dead at the entrance to the tower in circumstances which made it clear that he had been murdered while on his way to remove the identifiable part of his wife's corpse for burial.

No person was ever arrested for putting to death the murderous Menzies and the true circumstances of his death must be left to guesswork, but the recorded experience of two English guests staying in the castle in the year 1862, together with other experiences in living memory, confirm the reputed haunting of Meggernie Castle.

The two English guests were each given a large room in the tower which forms the oldest part of the castle. Before retiring for the night, one of them was fastening the door leading into his room from the hallway, when he noticed another door in the room which seemed to connect through to the room his friend occupied. The mystery door appeared to be sealed and without a keyhole. He managed to shout through to his friend and asked him if he also had a door on his side of the wall. His friend replied that a door in the same position on his side was in a small closet but the door appeared to be nailed or screwed up with no sign of a lock or keyhole.

They visited each other to see what the door looked like but, unable to explain the mystery, each went eventually to his own room and was soon fast asleep.

In the early hours of the morning the guest who first discovered the mystery door was awakened by the feeling of a hot kiss on his cheek, which seemed to burn through to the bone. As he jumped out of bed he saw the upper half of a woman's body floating away from his bedside and through the sealed door into the next room.

He rushed to the door expecting to be able to open it but found that it was just as securely sealed as before.

Finding the mystery door secure he then took up a lamp and went downstairs, but he did not see or hear anything unusual. He did not wish to disturb his friend in the adjoining room and so he returned to bed to await the daylight.

When daylight came he heard his friend stirring in the next room and called through the mystery door, saying that he had had a terrible night with little sleep. 'So have I,' replied his friend, who suggested that strange happenings had taken place in his room. Before they described their experiences to each other he said that he would give his version to an independent person.

Later the same day he described his experience to the person who was host to the two men. He stated that he was awakened by a strange light at about 2 AM and at the same time saw a female form at the foot of his bed. The form came along the side of the bed and bent over, but as the guest raised himself the form turned away and went into a small dressing room which had no windows and was built within the thick walls. The phantom figure appeared to be without legs and despite a search he found no trace of any intruder.

Needless to say the two men had their rooms changed for the next night.

According to local legend, about the year 1849 the remains of the head and shoulders of a dismembered female body were found under the floor of one of the tower rooms while repairs were being carried out on the castle. The bones were taken away and buried. It was thought then that the phantom would never be seen again, but the later experience of the two English guests confirmed that the haunting continued.

Within living memory, a local doctor from Aberfeldy who was attending a patient in the castle had to stay the night. The doctor was well aware of the phantom legend and the actual room in the tower had been pointed out to him on a previous visit. The doctor was lodged for the night in a room within the tower immediately below the legendary haunted room.

The doctor retired to rest on the bed, fully dressed and with the bedside light switched on. He thought that he might be called to attend to his patient during the night but, being tired out, he was soon asleep.

In due course the doctor was awakened by something which appeared to indicate that a person had entered the room. The bedside light was still burning but from his position in the bed the doctor was unable to see the door. On looking round the room he saw a human head and shoulders without body or legs move along one of the walls and then suddenly disappear. The doctor denied that his experience at Meggernie was in any way a nightmare; and if it was a dream it was the most vivid he had ever known.

The people of Glenlyon maintain that the haunting still takes place. Claims have also been made that the buried half of the body haunts the little graveyard in the castle park.

The Bodach Mor (Giant Old Man) of Ben Macdhui

Entering the district of Strathspey in Inverness-shire by the main road from Perth, the traveller descends from the high Drumochter pass into the valley of the river Spey. On the right are the dark Monadhliath mountains and on the left the range known as the Cairngorms.

Before reaching the village of Aviemore the visitor will skirt the shore of Loch Alvie where, on a narrow peninsula, stands the parish church of Alvie. A holy cell near the site of the church is said to have been founded by Saint Ailbhe, from whom the parish takes its name. The present church has undergone much re-building and alteration throughout its history.

About one hundred years ago alterations were being made to the church flooring when the workmen found one hundred and fifty human skeletons lying head to head under the old floorboards. The bones were transferred to the churchyard, where they were buried. The mystery has never been solved but it is said that a strange wailing is often heard at night sounding over the waters of the loch.

The highest mountain in the Cairngorm range is Ben Macdhui which is nearly 4,300 feet above sea level, making it the second highest mountain in Britain. The Spey is crossed by the new road bridge at Aviemore into Rothiemurchus. This road leads to Glenmore and the Cairngorm winter sports centre, where a large car park and chairlifts have been built.

Rothiemurchus was at one time part of the great Caledonian forest and remains of this forest can still be seen with the bare mountains in the background. Despite the number of visitors in summer and winter, one can still wander alone along the many ancient paths and cart tracks.

The 'robbers' road' at the back of Loch-an-Eilan is said to have been used by the famous Rob Roy and the ruined castle situated on an island in the loch is well worth a visit. But what of the Giant Old Man of Ben Macdhui?

The haunting is said to take place in the vicinity of the Larig Ghru pass which runs from Rothiemurchus to the Pool of Dee near Braemar. In ancient legend the

apparition was known as 'Am Famh' which can mean a giant or mole. The meaning mole is thought to describe the type of tracks left in the snow or soft ground. In 1864 the Bodach Mor was described as a ferocious giant frequenting the heights above the pass.

The mysterious creature sometimes known as the 'Yeti' or the 'Abominable Snowman' of the high Himalayas is well documented, as is the 'Wendigo' or 'Bigfoot' of North America. Tracks in snow have been seen and photographed.

The Yeti has been described as a large, long-armed, slouching ape-like creature adopting an upright posture and capable of running at speed over steep or rough ground. The skin of the creature is described as dark or grey, partly covered with reddish body-hair. The Yeti is said to have a face which is nearly human. As yet, no

one has photographed a Yeti or brought in a captive specimen or carcass for scientific examination. Many have professed knowledge of 'wild men' surviving in the high mountain regions of the world, and despite our modern civilization the evidence can not be entirely discounted.

One instance of the Bodach Mor's existence was given by a doctor climber who was on the top of Ben Macdhui with his brother. The doctor saw a figure which he took to be a man moving about close to where his brother was resting beside a cairn. The time was near to midnight and the figure seemed to be about ten feet tall. After wandering about, the figure seemed to turn down the mountain into the Larig Ghru pass.

On reaching the cairn where his brother was resting the doctor asked him if he had seen the strange figure. The brother claimed that he had not seen the stranger.

In 1925 another climbing enthusiast who was also a professor of organic chemistry was returning from the top of Ben Macdhui when he heard the crunching sound of footsteps behind him. Mist was falling at the time and on looking back he was unable to see anything. The professor was amused to think that the sound should disturb a man of his training; but the crunch-crunch continued and at last he was forced to surrender to blind terror. He ran, panic-stricken, to Glenmore Lodge with the certain knowledge in his mind that he had been followed by the Bodach Mor.

The Giant Old Man of Ben Macdhui has been the subject of discussion in Strathspey for many generations and several claims of sightings of the mystery figure have been made over the years.

Many stalkers, gamekeepers, and others who in the course of their daily work have to venture alone into the high mountains at all times of the day and night, claim that moonlit reflections on snow-covered ground or in hill mist cause figures to be magnified. On the other hand, many have experienced an awareness of something which cannot be explained in modern terms.

There is no doubt that people do believe that they have seen or heard something which cannot be explained in a rational way, but alone in the high and lonely places one *can* feel the sensation of being watched by unseen eyes.

The Police Station Haunting

Prior to the regionalization of the Scottish police force in 1973 each village of importance had its own police constable who was responsible for his area or beat on a 24-hour basis except for a weekly rest day; even then, if he was at his station, it was expected that he would take action on any crime or incident brought to his notice. The payment for overtime work was unknown except in some of the larger city forces.

The village constable was often assisted by his wife; and, in some respects, was in the same position as that of the parish minister, where the public obtained the services of two people (i.e. the minister and his wife) for the price of one.

The wife of a police officer in a country station was expected to take telephone messages and keep an open door for any member of the public who required assistance and information. In a small town the sergeant usually resided in a house at the police station, where accommodation was also provided for the inspector-in-charge and a senior police constable. Because he was always on the spot, it was possible at any time during the day or night for telephone messages to be received or attention given to a caller.

It will be appreciated that in these circumstances the local police were very much in contact with the public. Many of the wives were also involved in the feeding of the prisoners, searching female prisoners, and travelling people were sometimes grateful for a cup of tea or some outgrown children's clothing handed over by the wife of the village constable. In short, the police station was a focal point where advice and assistance were always available.

In one village there was a man who had a large family and who was inclined to drink to excess on a Saturday night. One of his usual actions while under the influence was to walk out of the house after a quarrel with his wife and threaten to drown himself in a nearby river. His behaviour caused his wife much distress and the village constable was called out to search for and bring Tam home to his bed. The weekly rest day for the constable *never* fell on a Saturday, one of his busiest days.

Arrest and a fine for a breach of the peace were out of the question, as any fine imposed would need to be paid from the weekly wages required to keep Tam's large family. In his wisdom, the local constable decided that some new and unusual type of punishment was necessary. The next time that his wife appeared at the police station to report that Tam was in a drunken mood causing her to leave home with the children, the constable accompanied her back to the house before Tam was able to leave for the riverside.

Part of the furniture in the living-room was a single iron bedstead with a mattress, and within a few seconds Tam found himself handcuffed by the wrist to the iron rail on the bed, where he had been placed by the constable, who was well over six feet in height and solidly built. Tam was told that he would be left handcuffed to the bed over the weekend in the charge of his wife, who seemed pleased to have Tam under her control.

By Sunday morning Tam's wife began to soften as she looked at her husband handcuffed helplessly to the bed. She called at the police station asking to have her husband released as he had promised to behave himself in future. Tam was duly released on making a tearful apology to the constable. The couple lived on to have 13 children, 49 grandchildren and 28 great-grandchildren. Such social work of twenty-four years ago might not be accepted today but in this case it was very effective.

*

Tragedy too has left its mark in many of the old police stations. In this respect the haunting of the house at one time occupied by the sergeant at Crieff Police Station in Perthshire is a very clear example. The wife of a sergeant stationed at Crieff died under tragic circumstances in the house situated above the office. She was a young Highland woman of a quiet nature and before her marriage was a receptionist at a well-known hotel in the Highlands.

Some time after the tragedy, between 1964 and 1965, this particular house at the police station was occupied by Sergeant John Gow, his wife and daughter Hazel, who was then about fourteen years of age. The first strange happening was during the hours of darkness, experienced by Sergeant Gow in a narrow passageway leading to the house, where he was conscious of what he took to be a person brushing past him.

He put the incident down to some trick of imagination and thought no more about it until some time

later when he and his wife were awakened in their bedroom by the family Corgi dog coming into the room growling as if in fright and retreating to hide under the bed. At the same time, distinct footsteps were heard coming up the stair to the bedroom, but no person appeared. Mr and Mrs Gow investigated thoroughly, finding only their daughter Hazel fast asleep and no other person in the house.

The footsteps were later heard on six to eight occasions over a period, sometimes about midnight or between 2 AM and 3 AM, when the sergeant and his wife were awakened once again by the sound of footsteps and the frightened behaviour of the family dog. On one occasion, when the bedside light was not switched on and the occupants lay listening in the dark, the sound of rustling papers was heard coming from the open bookcase in the bedroom where books and papers were stored. No figure of a person was ever seen and the footsteps always seemed to stop in the bedroom. The eerie experiences never caused any fear but were not told to their young daughter.

One strange coincidence did emerge at the breakfast table one morning when their daughter, Hazel, told her mother that she had awakened during the night and seen the figure of a tall woman dressed in a black silky dress standing in her bedroom and carrying a tray of glasses. The child claimed that she heard the glasses making a clinking sound when the woman walked away from the bedside and seemed to vanish through the wall of the room.

This is one case of a haunting where the facts are still remembered vividly by the participants.

The Ghosts of Loch Tayside

Crossing the hill road from the Bridge of Balgie in Glen Lyon to the north side of Loch Tay, a traveller is shadowed by Ben Lawers, which rises to about 4,000 feet. On leaving the shadow of the mountain the loch stands out clearly. It is flanked on the north side by the main road from Kenmore to Killin, with a backcloth of hills and hamlets on the south side.

Evidence of the depopulation of the district can be found along the north shore of the loch. At one time the principal mode of transport for both passengers and goods was by boat, and each of the little hamlets had its own pier. The entrance to the road leading to the pier at Lawers is situated on the main road between the school and Lawers Hotel. The road to the disused pier drops steeply to the side of the loch, where on the east side the ruins of a church and a small hamlet can be found. One of the houses, known as Ballivoulin, was sited close beside the ruined church. This house was once occupied by the Laird of Lawers, a man named Campbell, who was married to a Stewart of Appin in Argyllshire. This woman, who lived in the seventeenth century, was considered to be a prophetess and was known as *Ban-Tigheahran Lawer*, or in plain English 'The Lady of Lawers'.

It is said that this lady was responsible for having the church built about 1669 and it is intimately connected with many of her prophecies. When the church was being built she said that it would never be finished as the top stone would never be laid. She was right, for as this particular stone was being carried out of the boat at the pier it slipped from the hands of the workmen and was shattered to pieces. As a result, the correctly shaped stone *was* never laid, but in due course nevertheless the church was ready for use as a place of worship.

The Lady of Lawers planted an ash tree near the church on the day it was opened for worship and made a prophecy that, when the height of the tree reached that of the church spire, the days of the church would be finished. About 1831 the tree *did* reach the height of the spire and the church was so badly damaged by a thunderstorm that it had to be abandoned as a place of worship.

Many more of her prophecies came true. She said that iron vessels would sail on Loch Tay and that sheep would drive the crofters from the land. On the night the Lady of Lawers died, a great landslip occurred in the hills behind her home when the whole side of a hill went sliding into the channel of Lawers burn as though nature had been disturbed by her demise.

She had given instructions for her burial and said that out of her grave would spring a tree: any person who dared to cut the tree down would meet a violent death. She was buried as she desired, just outside the church where its walls formed an angle. As she had foretold, a tree *did* eventually grow out of her grave and it remained untouched as the local people remembered the prophecy and gave the tree a wide berth. However, between 1850 and 1855, the tenant of nearby Milton Farm, scorning the prophecy as idle superstition and acting against the advice of his friends and neighbours, cut down the tree. Shortly afterwards, in a field near the church and grave, his own Highland bull turned against him and gored him to death. This incident created a great sensation at the time. Part of that tree is now growing again, but I do not think it will be disturbed for a second time.

When wandering amid the ruined buildings by the lochside time seems to stand still, and one incident within recent years was experienced by Gwyn Price from Wrexham, who spent many of his days walking the highways and byways of Scotland. On one occasion he set out from Killin to walk the northern track for the purpose of visiting the grave of the Lady of Lawers. It was in the month of June at about eight o'clock in the evening when, having been walking in the sun all day, Gwyn was on the look-out for a place to rest and perhaps spend the night.

It was essential to find a place with a roof and this he managed to find in a field not far from the side of the loch. The house had been abandoned for some time and the door was ajar. In the silence of the evening before entering he heard a distinct thud coming from within the old house and was also conscious that he ought to say something in the Gaelic language, which in olden times was spoken throughout the area. It is possible that the required words would be *Am bheil cuid-eigen a stigh?* (Is there anyone in?)

As Gwyn stopped at the doorway of the room where he thought the sound came from, the compelling

requirement to speak in Gaelic became very strong, but having no knowledge of the language he remained silent. No voice or any other sound was heard as he entered, then suddenly in the supposedly empty room there appeared a number of women dressed in dark clothing and each had a cloth or shawl covering her head. They seemed to be bending over or working at an invisible table with their backs to the door of the room.

One of the women turned round to face the door and Gwyn could see that she was a teenage girl with a happy expression on her face and long fair hair falling out from under the headcloth which she wore. At the same time the figure of a tall well-built man dressed in a white shirt and a reddish-coloured kilt with yellow stripes seemed to appear from the wall on the right of the room and bend down at the disused fireplace. He appeared to do something with his hands, then stride away from the fireplace. As Gwyn looked back at the young girl, the kilted man disappeared and was replaced by two men who suddenly appeared at the far corner of the room. They were dressed in old grey suits and cloth caps of a fashion of about fifty years ago. Gwyn's inability to communicate seemed to have some effect and the whole scene vanished before his eyes.

The entire incident lasted for only a few minutes, and, as Gwyn was a little stunned by what he had seen, he did not enter further into the room but left the old house to spend the night in a shed at a nearby farm. The following morning he passed through Lawers village, having failed to locate the grave of the Lady of Lawers, and eventually made his way back home to Wales.

The Searching Woman of Lewis

The Western Islands of Scotland include about 500 islands of which only about one fifth are inhabited. The Isle of Lewis is the principal island, and its main town of Stornoway has a population of over 5,000 people. The airport at Stornoway has been extended and modernized within recent years but during the war years 1939 to 1945 it was an important Royal Air Force station covering the western approaches and the passage of shipping convoys round the north of Scotland. At Holm, near the entrance to Stornoway harbour, and at the Butt of Lewis in the extreme north, the Royal Air Force sited direction-finding units which were manned day and night. As members of these very small units, the airmen established friendships with the scattered crofting community.

The airmen came from all walks of life and in many respects they found the religion and habits of the local people somewhat strange. For example no work of any kind was carried out during the twenty-four hours of the Sabbath day when church service was the main activity. The men and women set aside all brightly coloured clothing and dressed in black for church. The various services of Holy Communion also extended over the greater part of one week in the church calendar.

Two airmen, Donald Paton and Charles Palmer –

who was known as 'Chick' to his pals – became friendly with an old widow-woman crofter by the name of Mrs MacLean. Her croft house overlooked the sea and she had many stories to tell of disaster at sea and a coastal shipwreck on the rocks at Holm when many Lewismen returning home from service in the First World War had lost their lives. The two airmen understood her way of life when she informed Donald on his first Sunday morning at the croft as he went to draw water from the well that it was the Sabbath day. Thereafter Donald obtained all the water for Sunday use late on Saturday night so as not to cause offence. The old woman appreciated the action of the young airman in complying with her wishes and not breaking the Sabbath.

One bright morning during the first week of September 1940, having obtained a 48-hour pass from the parent station at Stornoway, Donald and Chick decided that they would walk across the island and visit their airmen friends stationed at the Butt of Lewis. The air battles then being waged over the south of England seemed very far away, and by mid afternoon the two airmen had crossed the moors alongside the river Barvas to Loch Barvas where the high cliff ground was broken at a point where the sea rolled over a long stretch of golden sand.

After spending some time enjoying the scene and finishing a meal which they carried in their side packs, the two airmen decided it was time to resume the journey. No other person was to be seen and Chick pro-

duced his packet of cigarettes. At this point about fifty yards away the two airmen suddenly saw a woman approaching. She appeared to be middle aged and dressed in black clothing. They decided to wait and speak to the woman; having some difficulty in lighting their cigarettes in the wind blowing from the sea, they turned away. On looking up expecting the women to be nearby, they saw no sign of her. She seemed to have vanished as suddenly as she had appeared. There was certainly no place of concealment for the woman and the airmen were bewildered by what they had seen.

When first sighted the woman appeared to be looking for something by turning her head about. Donald and Chick waited, listening to the sound of the sea and wind. What had they seen? Both had heard about ghosts and goblins, but not in the twentieth century.

The strange experience made them anxious to be on their way and they took care to keep clear of a cemetery which was situated about a mile away from where they had seen the woman. They made no mention of what they had seen in case they were laughed at by their friends.

On their return to Holm, Mrs MacLean had prepared a meal for them and she was interested in their tour of the western side of the island, where she had been brought up as a child. In the course of conversation Donald decided to tell her about the strange sighting of the woman in black. He was expecting to be laughed at, but instead Mrs MacLean looked at him in sad silence and replied, 'That was Morag you saw.' It was then explained that in about 1895 a great storm arose and the husband of Morag, who was a shepherd, had been out tending his sheep. The shepherd failed to return by nightfall and Morag, who was anxious for his safety, had gone out of her croft house to look for him, leaving her children in the care of their old grand-mother.

The shepherd, who had sheltered in a cave during the height of the storm, arrived back home safe and sound with his two dogs, but his wife Morag never returned. Her body was never found and it was thought that she had been blown over a high cliff by the wind and swept out to sea. According to Mrs MacLean a number of local people from the Barvas area of Lewis had had the same experience as the two airmen.

Lady Greensleeves of Huntingtower

Huntingtower Castle is situated by the side of the main Perth-to-Crieff road about three miles from Perth. It was originally known as the House of Ruthven, until 1600 when the name was changed to Huntingtower by Royal Proclamation. The family of Ruthven had occupied the castle for about three hundred years and were involved in the episode known as 'The Raid of Ruthven' which took place in the summer of 1582, when the fourth Lord Ruthven, who had been created first Earl of Gowrie, and other Protestant nobles persuaded the young fifteen-year-old King James VI to accompany them to the House of Ruthven.

In fact, the young King was kidnapped and held by the Earl of Gowrie and his confederates for about ten months before he gained his freedom. Gowrie was forgiven by the young King for his part in the kidnap but in 1585 the Earl was ordered to leave the country. Before he managed to flee he was arrested in Dundee and charged with being party to a plot to seize Stirling Castle. He was beheaded at Stirling and his property forfeited to the Crown.

The estates and honours were restored in 1586 to his son James, who died when he was fourteen years of age. James was succeeded by his brother John, the third and last Earl of Gowrie. He and his brother Alexander were killed on 6 August 1600 in 'The House of Gowrie' in Perth for an alleged attempt on the life of the King. The incident, known as 'The Gowrie Conspiracy', is still shrouded in mystery. The third Earl – like his father and grandfather – was suspected of indulging in witchcraft and was said to have had the art of invoking the dead to foretell the future. The bodies were taken from Perth to Edinburgh, where they were hanged, quartered and drawn in the presence of the people, on the charge of high treason. The name of Ruthven was then abolished and remaining members pronounced incapable of succeeding or holding any honours or possessions.

Huntingtower, as it was then named, remained in Crown possession until 1643, when it passed into the hands of the Murray family and later into the family of Atholl. The building is now under the care of the Department of the Environment and is in good state of preservation.

The original Huntingtower (now the eastern tower) was a stone-built free-standing building with three storeys and a garret. Towards the end of the fifteenth century another independent tower of L-shaped structure was built, much the same in appearance as the first. A wooden bridge below the battlements connected the two towers. The eastern tower was then occupied mostly by servants and, if besieged and overrun, one tower could be defended by withdrawing the bridge. When the country became more settled, the space between the two towers was built up, creating the castle as it stands today.

The ghost of a tall young lady known as 'Greensleeves' is said to have been the daughter of the 1st Earl of Gowrie who was in love with a young man of inferior rank. By arrangement, the young man was in the habit of being lodged for the night in the servants' quarters at the top of the eastern tower while the family lived in the western tower. Unknown to her parents, the young lady visited her lover by way of the bridge connecting the two towers, but one of the servants reported the clandestine meeting to the old Countess. After receiving the information the Countess made her way over the bridge and so cut off any escape. The young lady heard the footsteps on the bridge and with all haste she made her way to the roof and battlements as the Countess entered the tower. Unable to return over the bridge, the young lady made a desperate leap of nine feet four inches over the chasm of sixty feet to land on the battle-

ments of the main tower and return to her own bed, where she was found by her mother, the Countess, after the unsuccessful search of the eastern tower.

It is said that the following night the couple eloped and were married. No further record can be found of what happened to the young couple but they certainly would not escape from the wrath of the cruel Earl and his wife.

The girl who made 'The Maiden's Leap' was said to be tall in stature with corn-yellow hair, wearing a mutch or head-coif and a dress with green silk-puff sleeves. Since the disappearance of 'The Lady Greensleeves' with her lover, the tall figure of a young woman dressed as described has been seen in the gloaming and sometimes in the full blaze of a noonday sun. The face of this woman is also alleged to have been seen at a window or windows of the castle. Some present-day visitors to the old tower claim that they can detect the smell of cooking.

Generally the appearance of 'Lady Greensleeves' foretold a calamity or death but she was also known to play the part of a benign guardian spirit. One incident recounted was that of a country girl who was waiting by the side of the nearby river Almond to meet her young farmer boyfriend. The young man was late and the girl sat down near a small clump of trees between the castle and the river. She had just sat down on that summer evening when she heard a voice saying, 'Look to the strand where the elms wave for there the lover may find his grave.' The girl then saw the figure of 'Lady Greensleeves' in the shadow of the trees and immediately ran home to her parents. It was then found that the young man who had left on horseback to meet the girl was missing and his horse had returned to the farm without the rider. Next morning the young man was found dead at the side of the river among some rocks with his head in a pool of congealed blood. It appeared that the horse had taken fright and thrown his rider.

In the early 1930s it is said that a commercial traveller who had stayed overnight with the then custodian at Huntingtower reported to his host of having seen 'Lady Greensleeves' in a passageway of the dwelling house attached to the castle and occupied by the custodian. The man was warned to stay clear of any danger during his journey the day following his sighting. After leaving Perth he travelled to Dundee in the course of business, and joined the ferry at Dundee to take him across to the Fife shore. During the journey he accidentally fell from the ferry boat and was drowned.

Another superstition surrounds the well to be found at the roadside beside Huntingtower Castle. The water from the well is said to have healing properties but the person who goes to collect the water must do so in complete silence and return with the water in the same manner. A small coin or charm must also be left at the well. A word spoken while on the journey to or from the well would break the charm and the water would be useless. The belief was so popular that on 21 April 1617 the Kirk Session at Perth made a rule prohibiting any of their congregation to go to the well at Huntingtower.

Hauntings at Glamis

There is probably no castle in Scotland more historically interesting than that of Glamis, where the swirling mists of history seem to enshroud the old towers and battlements. A legend frequently heard is that 'Fiery Pans' on the summit of nearby Hunter's Hill, where invasion warning beacons were set alight, was the site on which the castle was originally to be built. The builders set to work on this site but it was found that any progress made during the hours of daylight was mysteriously destroyed by some unseen hand during the night.

It was said that Hunter's Hill was the home of 'little people' who had been disturbed by the efforts of the builders. No progress was made until at dawn one fine summer morning a voice was heard to say 'Build the castle in a bog where it will neither shake nor shog.' As a result of this direction, believed to have come from the 'little people', the castle was built on the present site in the early years of the fifteenth century.

The castle is the seat of the Earls of Strathmore. It was also the Scottish home of the present Queen Mother and the birthplace of Princess Margaret. It is believed, despite the legend about the 'little people', that a fortified place occupied the site for centuries before the present castle was built.

Tragedy and legend are intertwined in many stories, along with the recorded experiences of guests and servants living in the castle at various times. The sudden death, about the year 1537, of the 6th Lord Glamis was said to have been caused by poisoning. His young wife Janet Douglas, a famous beauty, was accused of causing the death of her husband, but the evidence was inconclusive. About six years later Janet Douglas was found guilty on false evidence of plotting to murder King James of Scotland and was burned to death in Edinburgh. The estates were taken by the Crown from her young son but were restored after the death of the King.

Tragedy seemed to haunt the family until the late 1600s, when Patrick Lyon was made the 1st Earl of Strathmore. He made many alterations to Glamis and built into the structure a number of secret chambers which may have been considered as hiding places during these troubled times of Scotland. It is said that

during the march north to Aberdeen prior to the battle of Culloden in April 1746 the army of the Duke of Cumberland rested at Glamis; then, under the cover of darkness, local supporters of the rebellion cut some of the leather harness-girths of the army horses in an attempt to delay the march.

One legend of tragedy is that in 1821 a first-born son and rightful heir of the Earl was found to be deformed at birth and was kept out of sight from childhood to old age in one of the secret rooms because of his physical and mental deformities. To all intents and purposes this first-born son was said to have died in infancy and the closely guarded secret was known only to the successive heirs and faithful factors of the estate. A contributor to a magazine in 1880 wrote that a workman who had been carrying out structural alterations inadvertently put a crowbar through what he thought was a solid wall only to discover a secret corridor leading to a locked door. The man became frightened and reported on what had happened. The Earl, who was in London at the time, was summoned home by his factor and it is said that the workman and his family immediately emigrated to Australia and were never heard of again.

One appearance which may be linked to the secret room has been described as the form of an old person with crooked misshapen legs and a large head with a tangled mass of grey hair. One lady claimed that she had been awakened one night by the feel of a beard or mass of hair brushing over her face.

In the present Royal Apartments there is a little stone seat just inside the door of the sitting room, and it is said that a little ghostly figure has been seen sitting on the seat and then disappearing through the wall. Another is a tall figure clad in bright armour who is usually seen in the Square Tower and is associated with a noise like the clashing of swords as if a fight with weapons were taking place.

One bright moonlit night a guest looking from a window saw a dark object moving down the avenue towards the castle; as it came nearer he saw it was a carriage pulled by two horses, but there was no sound of wheels as it pulled up at the main door. After about a minute it drove silently away and the driver looked up. The onlooker saw that the driver had a terrible marked face which he felt he should never forget. At breakfast in the morning the guest remarked to the

Earl of Strathmore that he must have had a very late visitor arriving in the carriage. The guest was given no explanation by the Earl, who became agitated and the subject was changed. Shortly after his visit to Glamis the same guest was about to enter a lift while staying in a Paris hotel when he saw in the lift a man whom he identified as the driver of the carriage. He stepped back from the lift in fright and in an instant there was a mighty crash as the lift fell to the ground floor.

The most recent sighting of a carriage at Glamis was during 1979 between 4 AM and 5 AM when a 38-year-old lorry driver, Donald Martin, was driving alone in a motor lorry carrying a full load of bottled milk in crates.

His usual route from his depot was through the village of Meigle on the main A94 road, then turning in towards Glamis village to join the A928 road to Kirriemuir directly opposite the main entrance gates of Glamis Castle. On turning left opposite the gates, the Kirriemuir road is bounded on the right by a wall. About two hundred yards along this road before coming to double bends Donald Martin had to brake his lorry suddenly as a carriage pulled by two horses emerged from an opening in the wall and crossed the road from right to left. No noise was heard as the carriage disappeared. It was described as an open vehicle with passengers sitting along the sides facing each other, it was larger than the old-fashioned governess carriage, with the door and steps at the rear. The backs of the passengers on one side were seen by the lorry driver but in the flash of time he was unable to describe the driver of the carriage.

The ghostly carriage was seen on two more occasions resulting in Donald's taking another route to Kirriemuir by turning off the main road before entering the village of Meigle. He was afraid that the sudden application of the brakes might shift his load of milk crates. His last sighting was in November 1979, and by avoiding the vicinity of Glamis the milk has been delivered safely to Kirriemuir ever since.

Scottish Poltergeists

Supernatural molestations, fearful noises, the moving of furniture or ornaments, the throwing of stones and pins being put into foodstuff were – in the early days – considered to be the work of witches who were able to go about unseen or change into an animal. The cat was said to be a favourite form for transformation.

The story is told about a witch who lived in the parish of Laggan, Inverness-shire. One day a young gamekeeper working in the Gaick forest sought shelter in a bothy house near a spring known as the Duke of Gordon's Well. He was accompanied by his black Labrador dog and managed to kindle a fire in the bothy grate with the dry sticks which were always kept inside the building.

The young gamekeeper was about to settle down until the heavy rain stopped when he heard a strange scratching sound and his dog appeared to be in fear, with the hair on its back standing up. On opening the bothy door, assisted by a very strong gust of wind, the gamekeeper was surprised to see a large black cat which came through the door and sprang up on to a shelf above the bothy fireplace. Seeing the cat, the dog seemed to recover from its fright and it was only with difficulty that the gamekeeper managed to keep it from attacking the strange cat.

Eventually the dog settled down at the other end of

the bothy and the cat came down from the shelf to sit in front of the fire. The fur of the cat was very wet and the heat of the fire seemed to make steam rise from its coat. The steam increased and the gamekeeper saw that in the midst of this volume of steam the cat was changing into the form of a woman whom he identified as a neighbour from the village of Laggan.

The dog became enraged by this change from cat to woman and it sprang forward, sinking its teeth into the woman despite the efforts of the gamekeeper, who had opened the bothy door and tried to force the dog outside. When the dog attacked, the woman changed back into the form of a cat and with the use of its claws and teeth managed to escape through the open door – leaving a trail of blood.

When the rain was over the young gamekeeper made

his way home after attending to the injuries received by his dog. Arriving home he told his wife of what had happened, naming the woman he had seen in the bothy. His wife then told him that the woman in question had suddenly taken ill that day during the rain storm and was not expected to survive.

With a view to satisfying himself he went to the woman's house, where he found that a number of the neighbours had gathered. He told the villagers of what had happened in the forest bothy and, when the bedclothes were pulled aside, large bite marks could be seen on the woman's legs. In her agony the woman admitted that she was a witch. The neighbours then went away and left her to die.

*

One of the first recorded poltergeist activities was from the village of Glenluce in Galloway in a house occupied by a family named Campbell. It was said that a beggar came to the door one day asking for money and was refused. Within a few days after the visit from the beggar – who cursed the family for their refusal – strange whistling noises were heard within the house, stones were hurled through the windows and the bedclothes were pulled from the cots of the sleeping Campbell children.

The children were sent away to stay with relatives and all was quiet until one of the children, named Tom, had to return home due to illness. The strange manifestations started as soon as Tom returned to the family home. A voice was heard purporting to be that of the spirit involved, who blamed witches for his state and requested that a spade be brought and a grave dug for the wandering spirit.

Local ministers from churches in the district were told of the voice and they gathered in the house to hear the voice for themselves. One minister suggested that the voice spoke out of the boy Tom. The spirit seemed to take offence at this suggestion and before the eyes of the assembled company a naked hand and arm appeared in the room, beating on the floor until the foundations shook. It was believed by the villagers that the beggar who had cursed the family was responsible and in fact the manifestations only ceased when the beggar was later hanged for a crime he had committed.

Another recorded case was in 1718 at the manse of Rev. McGill, minister in Kinross; in addition to stone-throwing and knocking, bread cooked by the minister's

wife was found to contain pins. On one occasion, the girl employed as a maid at the manse became violently sick after eating some meat, and vomited up five pins. The minister's Bible was thrown into the household fire. For some reason the Bible would not burn but a pewter plate and two silver spoons thrown into the fire at the same time melted immediately. The Bible was recovered from the ashes and the manifestations ceased.

*

Poltergeist manifestations are well known to the present day, the only difference being that witches are not now held to be responsible. But even today there are points of similarity between the very old recorded instances such as repeated tappings, furniture dragged about, ornaments moved from place to place and the hearing of a voice or voices which sometimes reveal themselves as spirits of the dead.

In 1974 two young nurses who were working together in Dundee managed to find a furnished flat which they intended to share but were forced to leave within days due to frightening experiences. One of the girls was awakened during the night by the figure of an old woman bending over her bed. The figure was outlined by a street lamp shining through the bedroom window and the woman spoke in a soft menacing voice. The young nurse switched on her bedlight only to discover that the room was empty. At first she thought that she might have been dreaming, but she was unable to sleep; when her friend, who was on night duty, returned in the morning they discussed what had happened.

They had both heard strange tapping noises but not

when they were in the flat together. Two days later they were both in the flat when one of the girls heard a noise as if someone was in the kitchen. On hearing the noise she tapped on the wall dividing her bedroom from the kitchen, knowing that by arrangement the other girl would tap back on the wall to give reassurance that all was well. Instead of the arranged friendly tap from the kitchen there was a great outburst of noise as if someone was trying to break through the brickwork. It so happened that the other girl had been in the bathroom and on hearing the loud noise ran into the bedroom where her friend was standing horrorstruck. The two friends fled from the building and never returned to the haunted tenement house.

The present occupants of the tenement house have never been troubled by any strange happenings, but it is significant that the tenement building was erected on the site of a former mental asylum.

*

One elderly lady recalls her childhood in a farm cottage at Strowan near Comrie in Perthshire. The house has now been demolished and further research is impossible, but she remembers objects being moved within the house and the main experience, or manifestation, involved the main door of the house. It was a double door, one side being secured by an iron bar and hook with a strong heavy lock on the other side.

According to the old lady the main double door often burst open when the house was unoccupied after being left secure and locked. Neighbours were also disturbed as the door very often opened with a loud crash. In one instance all the family left the house after making the door secure, and neighbours agreed to watch and see what happened. The family had travelled only about fifty yards down the road to another road junction when a loud crash was heard. They returned immediately to find the double door standing wide open. The watching neighbours confirmed that no person had been seen when the door crashed open.

Comrie is situated in a Scottish earthquake area, but this certainly did not cause the door to burst open in the presence of witnesses.

*

Another instance slightly comparable to the Dundee case was that of two young schoolteachers who also occupied a furnished house. The bed in which one of the teachers was sleeping was found to have moved to a different position in the bedroom during the night. You can imagine the feelings of the young teacher in the morning on wakening to find her bed in a different position from when she went to sleep!

The teachers discussed the strange happening but were not in any way afraid. The one involved with the bed movement – which had happened a second time – suggested that she might change her room. Her companion, who came from the Isle of Harris, suggested that she should sleep with a Bible under her pillow. This was done and the bed never moved again.

There are two common features in all poltergeist hauntings. The first being that the families or persons troubled appear to have been devout and caring persons. The second and more important is that the troubled person was mostly young or a child-medium. It is a physiological fact that many children closely resemble their grandparents rather than their immediate parents, and it was believed by primitive man that the spirits of deceased ancestors took up their abode in the new-born infant.

Don Juan

Charles Campbell of Kinloch in Strathbraan, near Amulree, Perthshire, was forced to flee from Scotland because of his support for the Jacobite cause against the wishes of his family. He travelled to Portugal, where he made another mistake by eloping with a charming young lady who was related to the Bishop of Oporto. The clandestine marriage took place across the Spanish border.

The couple returned to Portugal but the marriage was not accepted, and they were banished to Brazil after making a promise that a second son, if born, would be educated for the Roman priesthood. In Brazil the couple brought up six children, four boys and two girls. When the second son Gregory came of age he was sent to study in Portugal under the control of the Bishop of Oporto.

It was reported that Gregory had been drowned at sea while on a voyage carrying him to study in Rome. The report of the drowning was later found to be false but the Bishop urged Charles Campbell to send the next-born son, named John, to take the place of the missing Gregory. Despite protest John, then eighteen years of age, was shipped off to Oporto. The mother and fourth son died in Brazil, where one daughter married and the other became a nun.

After the death of his wife, Charles Campbell returned to Strathbraan with his oldest son Joseph to claim his heritage as Laird of Kinloch. His third son, John, gave up the priesthood and obtained a commission in a Scottish Highland regiment serving in the Low Countries. He found this to be even more of a martyrdom than the priesthood, especially the wearing of Highland dress. He left the regiment and went to live with his father and brother at Kinloch.

Charles Campbell died in strange circumstances about 1795 not long after establishing his inheritance. It happened that the two sons went on a visit to a family living near Aberfeldy, leaving the old Laird alone at Kinloch. During the evening a messenger arrived to inform the sons that their father had taken seriously ill. Joseph and John made their way home in the darkness and on arrival at Kinloch House learned that two priests had arrived from the Crieff district. The priests had taken over complete charge from the servants in the sick room and refused to open the door for the two sons. It was not until Joseph had summoned the local blacksmith to force the door that it was opened from the inside. By this time the Laird was dead.

The Laird was buried with the full rites of the, then outlawed, Church of Rome; but, in the presence of all those gathered at the funeral, the two sons renounced the Catholic faith. Joseph became Laird of Kinloch. He never married and was more akin to his father's people, while John had all the appearance of his mother and was known locally as Don Juan. He cut a handsome figure. He tied his hair with a bunch of black ribbons at the back of the high collar of his claret-coloured cutaway coat with its large gilt buttons. He wore a soft muslin neckerchief, a frill of delicate lace down the front of his shirt and lace ruffles at the wrists, combined with black knee-breeches, silk stockings and silver-buckled shoes. Out of doors he was never seen without a loose Spanish cloak with silver clasps, one end flung over his left shoulder, and always wore a wide-brimmed hat. Don Juan also carried a tall gold-topped cane of Brazilian wood.

Years went by and one night in winter a great storm swept down Strathbraan and around Kinloch House. The two brothers were alone with the servants in their quarters when a loud banging noise was heard coming from the front of the house. It was thought at first that the high wind might have blown down the heavy branch of a tree. Joseph did not want to disturb the servant so he took a lantern and went to the front door with his brother. As the latch of the door was raised the wind flung open the door and extinguished the lantern. At the same time the tall dark figure of a man in a long cloak came through the door and into the passage beyond.

John, who was struggling to close the door against the wind, did not see the face of the stranger as Joseph took him straight into his private room on the ground floor. A manservant was called to bring food and drink into the private room. This servant was also instructed to inform Mr John not to wait up but to go to bed, as the Laird would attend to the gentleman who had arrived. This was the last instruction the Laird ever gave, as he was never seen alive again.

John was uneasy about the instructions he had received but went upstairs to his bed confident that the

stranger must be known to his brother. As dawn was breaking over the hills after the storm, a wild shriek was heard coming from the private room where the Laird had gone with the stranger. The shriek awakened the whole household and John, with two manservants, rushed into the private room only to find the Laird dead in his chair. His silver drinking cup was upset on the table beside the chair and a door leading from the room into the garden was open. The mysterious stranger had disappeared; it looked as if he had made a hurried exit into the garden.

John believed that his brother had been murdered, but the authorities were not convinced that a crime had been committed despite the fact that the mysterious stranger was never traced. John reluctantly took over the estate and spent a great deal of his time searching about the country for the supposed murderer of his brother. John or Don Juan was well known in Perth, where some of his relatives were merchants. He eventually married Ann Campbell of Melfort in 1804 but up to that time he continued to dress in Portuguese or Spanish fashion with a large broad-brimmed hat and cloak and carrying his tall cane.

It is said that a figure is sometimes seen in car headlights by motorists travelling through Strathbraan. The figure seems to melt away into woodland at the roadside but the dress is always described as a long dark cloak. One summer evening in 1936 a young girl named Ann was playing at an entrance leading to the house of a relative in Princes Street, Perth, when she suddenly saw a person standing at the end of a lane leading to an

old tenement building on the opposite side of the street. No other person was about at the time. The person she saw had a thin face, sallow complexion and was of medium height. The dress of the person was very striking and consisted of a long black cloak with one end over the shoulder and a large broad-brimmed hat. He carried a light sword or cane. The figure was only visible for a minute or so and then seemed to vanish into thin air. The girl was not upset and did not tell anyone else of having seen the figure.

In November 1978 Ann, now married to a local businessman, employed a new daily help and as usual the conversation turned to where their respective parents and relatives had lived in Perth. Anne explained that her relatives had lived in Princes Street opposite a lane leading to tenement buildings which had now been demolished to make way for a metered parking place. The daily woman then said that when she was about fifteen years old she had had a chum who lived in the now-demolished tenement. She also said that one night she was climbing the stairs to her friend's house when a man dressed in a long black coat and a broad-brimmed hat carrying a cane or something in his hand passed her going down the stairs. On reaching the house she asked her friend's mother about the man in the funny clothes she had seen. The mother replied, 'Oh, it's all right, that's just the Spanish ghost.'

Anne was startled to receive this information and a description which coincided exactly with what she had seen in the same area years before. Could it have been 'Don Juan' still hunting for the supposed murderer of his brother?

Common Hauntings

According to the available information it might appear that hauntings are more likely to take place in old castles or stately homes. In fact, the odds are that hauntings most often occur in ordinary homes or modest dwellings. The ghostly figure or figures in such cases are liable to be quite unremarkable. The reason why old castles or mansions appear to be in the forefront is the fact that the happenings in such places are well-recorded over long periods while in a more humble dwelling the sightings are not given the same publicity. In general, such humble ghostly figures are more often benevolent rather than malevolent, and take many guises.

For example, Mr and Mrs Crombie lived in a ground-floor flat forming part of a building in the Morningside district of Edinburgh for a period of two years from 1975 to 1977. The building was erected about 1900 and the ground-floor flat occupied by the Crombie family had a large hallway with other rooms leading from it.

One morning Mrs Crombie was using her electric vacuum cleaner in the hallway when a woman aged about forty, of medium build, with light brown hair and wearing a tweed suit and heavy outdoor shoes in the fashion of the 1930s suddenly appeared without a sound. With a hurrying gait the figure walked towards the main outside door and appeared to vanish through the door without opening it. No feeling of fear was experienced and during 1976 the woman in the tweed suit was seen three times while Mrs Crombie was alone in the house. Her husband and other members of the family never saw the woman or experienced anything unusual in the house.

*

A similar experience happened to a young married woman living in an old house in the main street of a village in central Scotland. She tells of an elderly man with one arm who suddenly appeared sitting in her armchair at the fireside. No conversation was made and, after two or three minutes, the old man rose from the chair and seemingly vanished into thin air.

The young woman did not have any fear of what she had seen, and a woman of eighty-three years of age who had spent her childhood in the village recalled that an old man who lived near that particular house was an ex-soldier who had only one arm. It was thought that he had lost his arm while serving with a Highland regiment in India.

The young woman was always alone in the house when the old man appeared but her husband was confident that the happenings – which took place on more than one occasion – were believable. After moving to a council house in the next village the young woman received no more unusual visitors.

*

Another incident took place some years ago in a tenement house in High Street, Rutherglen, near Glasgow. The family consisted of a mother, father, maternal grandmother and three young children. In such tenement houses the living room contained two main features, a built-in bed recess and a large fireplace which incorporated an oven on one side and a hot water tank on the other, with a brass tap for drawing the hot water; both heated from the coal fire. The fire had a hob on each side; but, by pulling out a flat iron section over the fire, a continuous hob was formed. A hinged door at the front could shut and cover the fireplace ribs. Due to this construction, considerable noise was made while a person was attending to the fire.

The maternal grandmother was in the habit of attending to the fire late at night and disturbing the sleeping children. This caused some upset in the family and the grandmother decided to leave and go to stay with a relative in Australia. She found that after a few months she did not like the new country but she was unable to return to Scotland. In every letter to her daughter she expressed the wish that some day she might be able to return to their home in Rutherglen.

The old lady had been in Australia for about two years when her daughter in the High Street tenement was awakened early one morning by what she thought was somebody working at the fireplace with a poker. In the first light of the early morning, from her position at the front of the recess bed she saw the figure of her mother working at the fireplace but no noise was to be heard. The figure suddenly vanished and the daughter, whose husband was working on a night shift at a local factory, arose and made herself a cup of tea. She also saw that the time on the wall clock was 4.30 AM. The young wife later received a letter from the relative in

Australia to say that her mother had died. The date and time of death as given in the letter coincided exactly with that moment in the early morning when the figure of her mother had been seen at the fireside.

Some may claim that the incident in the High Street tenement was, in fact, extrasensory perception, known as ESP, or thought transference involving part of the brain called the cerebellum. It is also said that the greater the distance between the 'transmitter' and 'receiver' the stronger is the experience.

Space People

During the Second World War the airmen of all the nations involved reported strange disc-shaped objects following their aircraft or flying alongside which would suddenly vanish at very high speed. Within recent years hundreds of such sightings by people on the ground have been reported from France and North America. Scotland has had its fair share of unidentified flying objects, and in one case the round, disc-shaped object was seen to hover and stop at about ground level on an open field during the early hours of the morning. The object then lifted off and disappeared after two or three minutes.

The two occupants of a nearby bungalow who saw the object went to the same part of the field at first light but failed to find any marks on the grass or other evidence to suggest that the object had actually landed.

Some of the sightings in Scotland have been traced to electrical storms over the hills or large inland lochs where lighting is conducted over high ground and then seen to bounce like a dambuster bomb over the flat surface of the water. Other sightings are unexplainable and the question of the objects being manned by living persons or intelligent creatures from other inhabited worlds has been under consideration for many years.

In Russia and also in the West scientists claim to have received radio signals from outer space, but the problem of separating such signals from natural pheno-

mena has yet to be solved. Scientists in the main are careful not to publish findings without the full study of all available evidence as they have often been proved wrong when further evidence is brought to light. For example, a scientific commission reported to the British government in 1878 that it would be impossible to adapt electric lighting for household purposes as it would be 'contrary to the laws of the universe'. In addition to such lighting we now have television and spaceships to 'defy the laws of the universe' – who can say what might happen in the next hundred years?

It has been found that strange unexplained happenings in childhood remain as a picture in the mind well into old age, while usual childhood memories are easily forgotten. One such happening is reported by a middle-aged woman who, as a girl of about eleven years of age, was on her way home from a Stirlingshire village school on a winter afternoon. In the falling dusk she was walking along a lonely road by the side of the river Avon when she suddenly saw a figure cross the road in front of her and disappear into the woods.

The sight of the strange figure remained as a picture in her mind; as a mature woman she described the figure as being of medium size and wearing clothing which looked like an old-fashioned diver's suit with a large round helmet. A number of sketches were produced for the woman from information received from witnesses in the United States of America who were alleged to have seen strange figures of personnel connected with UFOs, and she immediately picked out one wearing what could be described as a diving suit with a large round helmet and heavy footwear.

The Mystery Islands

The sea has held a fascination for man ever since his first raft or dugout canoe managed to float and sail on the waves, carrying him to neighbouring island shores. The early civilizations of Greece and Rome had their own sea gods, and the Norse or Scandinavian raiders brought much of their sea lore to Scotland. The Viking raiders left their mark on the northern and western islands including Iona, which was uninhabited when St Columba landed in 563 AD.

According to a middle-aged master joiner, who as a young man and member of the Iona community was assisting to restore the ancient abbey buildings, it was alleged by another member of the community that on a moonlit night while walking on the shore at a place known as White Sands he saw a phantom fleet of Viking longboats approaching the island. His story was put down to imagination and listening to local folklore, but it is an historical fact that Vikings did land at White Sands in the late eighth century and after murdering a number of the monks set fire to the settlement.

Due to the Viking raids, a settled monastic life became impossible and the remaining monks moved to the safety of Kells in Ireland. The community eventually returned and started to build in stone to replace the small beehive-shaped cells made of timber and turf. Iona was the burial place of the Scottish Kings into the

eleventh century, Duncan and Macbeth being among those reported as having been buried there. It is said that in three large tombs forty-eight Scottish Kings, four Irish Kings and eight Norwegian Kings were buried.

The narrow strip of sea known as the Sound of Iona can be crossed by ferry from Iona to Fionnphort on the island of Mull, which is the largest of the Inner Hebrides. In the south-east of Mull at the head of Loch Buie are Lochbuie House and the ruins of Castle Moy standing in the shadow of Ben Buie. The MacIaines occupied the lands for over 500 years and the last of the family to reside at Lochbuie House was the 22nd Laird, who won fame as a soldier in the First World War.

They were a younger branch of the Macleans of Duart.

The ghost of the headless horseman is associated with the Chief of the MacIaines. According to legend, Ewen, the only son of the Chief, who was under the influence of his wife, turned against his father and gathered together some clan supporters to fight his father for possession of the Loch Buie lands.

On the day before his battle for the lands Ewen is said to have been told by a woman he found washing a bundle of bloodstained clothing at a burn that if butter appeared on his table the following day without his having to ask for it he would win the battle but if no butter appeared he would be defeated. Next morning Ewen sat down to breakfast before setting out with his followers, but no butter appeared on the table. Undaunted, Ewen set out, and he found his father's force already in a strong position by the side of Loch Uisg with a supporting force under the command of his uncle Maclean of Duart.

In an attempt to rally his followers Ewen made a mounted charge on his black stallion. A claymore flashed from behind a high rock. The horse continued the charge and on its back was seen the headless body of Ewen. The sight of their headless leader caused his followers to turn and flee. It is claimed that a headless horseman is to be seen in the glen where the battle took place and even in recent years the sound of a galloping horse has been heard on a clear winter's night.

*

As man's knowledge of the sea grew, so did his fears as he extended his journeys into the unknown. Tales were heard of monsters from the deep such as giant sea serpents or the kelpie of Scottish folklore. The kelpie takes on the disguise of a horse and is said to lurk by the side of certain Scottish deep-water sea lochs. It has been generally accepted that a monster seen and photographed in Loch Ness has yet to be properly identified, and 1974 expeditions with sonar equipment have attempted to trace a similar monster in Loch Morar.

In addition to the phantom longboats of Iona many residents of the Western Isles claim to have heard strange calls coming from the sea like the voice of one crying desperately for help. From the island of Barra, which forms part of the Outer Hebrides, there are authenticated folktales of human cries coming from the sea. Another case may be the disappearance of three keepers from the lighthouse on the Flannan Isles in the North Atlantic about twenty-six miles out from Lewis. On the night of 15 December 1900 a ship reported that the Flannan light on Eilean Mor had not been seen. Due to stormy weather the lighthouse relief ship was unable to reach Eilean Mor until eleven days later. A search was made but no trace could be found of the three keepers, who were all experienced men. The ashes in the lighthouse fireplace were cold and the last entry on a slate was made at 9 AM on 15 December showing certain barometric readings, but no more. Many lighthouse keepers to this day claim that voices from the sea, perhaps in distress, had lured the keepers on to the rocks where they had been swept away by the stormy sea.

Notes

The Ghosts of St Andrews
The stories related are only a few of the recorded instances in the local history of St Andrews.

The Ghost of Inverawe
The Ticonderoga story is one of the legends of the Black Watch Regiment. Fort Carillon, where Major Duncan Campbell received the wound which caused his death three days later, was the name given to it by the French. It is said that the waters running from Lake George and Lake Champlain reminded them of the pealing of bells. Major Campbell was buried near the scene of the action.

The fostering of male children was a feature of the Highlands. Children of three or four years of age were sent to foster parents under agreements which provided for a supply of cattle or goods for his upkeep. The system formed a strong link between foster brothers. For example, the child of a laird or chief was fostered with ordinary folk. He then became aware of the lives of the common people, which helped him to manage his estate when he came of age.

On the other hand a clever child of poor parents was often fostered by the laird or chief and given an education which enabled many to reach high positions in the land.

It is said that on the night Duncan Campbell died, in July 1758, his ghost, dressed in the uniform of an officer of the 42nd Highlanders, appeared at Inverawe; and this Highland officer is still said to haunt the district.

Further information on the house of Inverawe is contained in *Argyll, the Enduring Heartland* by Marion Campbell and published in 1977 by Turnstone Press Ltd.

Barking Dogs

John Gillies, crofter and boat hirer of Morar, along with other local people claims to have seen the monster in Loch Morar. Various other sightings are recorded in *Search for Morag* by Elizabeth Montgomery Campbell and David Solomon and published in 1972 by Tom Stacey Ltd. The last reported sighting in the book was on 10 August 1971.

The Cape Wrath Ghost

This is a local legend and is similar in many ways to that of the Searching Woman of Lewis.

Green Ladies

The ghosts of Green Ladies seem to abound in Scotland and the stories given are taken from local legend. The story of the Stirling Castle ghost is connected with the Argyll and Sutherland Highlanders, who have their regimental museum in the castle.

Ghosts of Inchnadamph

Taken from local legend and newspaper reports.

The Haunting at Vicars Bridge
The author has personal experience of incidents at the bridge.

The White Lady of Castle Huntly
Information obtained from Longforgan Parish records and ex-member of staff.

The Ghost of Meggernie Castle
The two English guests referred to are named, under the title 'The Ghost in Two Halves', in *Fifty Great Ghost Stories* edited by John Canning and published by Souvenir Press Ltd.

The Bodach Mor (Giant Old Man) of Ben Macdhui
A well-known local legend. Information obtained from old residents of Aviemore. The book *Fifty Strange Stories of the Supernatural*, edited by John Canning and published by Souvenir Press Ltd, tells of a troop of Boy Scouts who had a strange experience in the Cairngorms involving a grey-clad giant man.

The Police Station Haunting
The Gow family are still alive but the house in question is no longer occupied by a member of the police force.

The Ghosts of Lochtayside
Information was contained in a written report sent to the author by Gwyn Price of Wrexham.

The Searching Woman of Lewis
Donald M. Paton Sr is resident in Perth but his com-

panion Charles Palmer who can corroborate the incident has emigrated to Australia.

Lady Greensleeves of Huntingtower

Huntingtower Castle is held in trust for the nation by the Secretary of State for Scotland and cared for on his behalf by the Department of the Environment. Ruthven was the family name and William, the fourth Lord Ruthven, was created Earl of Gowrie in 1581. As a result of the Gowrie Conspiracy in 1600 an Act of Parliament abolished the surname Ruthven and changed the name of the castle to Huntingtour or Huntingtower as it is known today. The estate was in the hands of the Crown for a second period from 1600 to 1643 when it passed into the hands of the Murray family. The well at the roadside is still running clear.

Hauntings at Glamis

Elliot O'Donnell, a serious investigator of the occult, who died in Bristol in 1965 at the age of ninety-five years, tells in his book *Scottish Ghost Stories*, published by Jarrold Colour Publications, Norwich, of having seen the ghost of the deformed rightful heir while staying at Glamis Castle. The witness Martin is very positive about what he saw.

Scottish Poltergeists

The old road through Gaick forest called Rathad nan Cuimeinach – Road of the Comyns – appears to have had an evil reputation not equalled anywhere else in the Highlands. It is aptly described in the words of a Gaelic poet of the eighteenth century: 'Black Gaick of the wind-whistling, crooked glens, ever enticing her admirers to their destruction'.

Further information on the Glenluce poltergeist known as the Glenluce Devil is contained in *Fifty Strange Stories of the Supernatural* edited by John Canning.

The farm cottage at Strowan near Crieff has been demolished but the elderly lady who recalled her childhood at the cottage is still alive.

Don Juan

The story of Don Juan is a legend of Perthshire and the two persons who speak of seeing the Spanish Ghost in the vicinity of Princes Street, Perth, are still alive.

Common Hauntings

The research in this respect has taken the author away from castles and stately homes. The witnesses are all credible.

Space People

Information on alleged sightings of Space People is contained in the book *Alien Intelligence* by Stuart Holroyd (1979), published by David & Charles (Publishers) Ltd, Newton Abbot, Devon.

The Mystery Islands

In addition to ancient legends and the sighting of Viking longboats in the gathering mist on the shore of Iona, the nearby island of Staffa provides the awe-inspiring Fingal's Cave immortalized by Mendelssohn in his Hebridean Overture.

Glossary of Scottish Terms

Aiver, an old horse
Aizle, a hot cinder

Bairn, a child
Bannock, oatcake
Baudron, a cat
Bield, shelter
Biggin, a house
Bing, a heap of coal, etc
Birkie, a clever fellow
Blether, to talk idly
Bock, to vomit
Breeks, trousers
Burn, small stream

Carl, an old man
Carlin, an old stout woman
Clachan, a small village
Clavers, idle stories
Clishmaclaver, idle conversation
Clootie, an old name for the Devil
Coof, a blockhead
Couthie, kind, loving

Dight, to wipe
Droukit, wet

Eerie, frightened, dreading spirits

Fash, to care for
Forfoughten, fatigued

Gawky, half-witted
Glen, a dale, a deep valley
Gowk, a cuckoo; a term of contempt
Grozet, a gooseberry

Haggis, a kind of pudding, boiled in the stomach of a sheep
Hirple, to walk with limp, to creep

Jink, to dodge
Jouk, to stoop

Keek, to peep
Kintra, country
Kirk, church

Loof, the palm of the hand
Lug, the ear

Midden, a dunghill

Nieve, a fist

Pech, short of breath, as in asthma
Pow, the head

Rax, to stretch
Reek, smoke

Sark, a shirt
Shachled, distorted, shapeless
Skelp, to slap
Snash, abuse
Snood, a ribbon for binding the hair
Sough, a heavy sigh
Sprackle, to clamber
Spurtle, a stick used in making pudding, etc
Stirk, a year-old bullock
Stoiter, to stagger
Swatch, a sample

Tocher, marriage portion

Unskaith'd, unhurt

Wame, belly
Water Kelpies, monsters in the guise of horses
Waukrife, not apt to sleep
Whigmeleeries, whims, fancies
Wraith, a spirit or ghost

Yett, a gate

Older Piccolo fiction you will enjoy

○	**Deenie**	Judy Blume	£1.25p
○	**It's Not the End of the World**	Judy Blume	£1.25p
○	**Tiger Eyes**	Judy Blume	£1.25p
○	**Scottish Hauntings**	Grant Campbell	£1.25p
○	**The Gruesome Book**	Ramsey Campbell	£1.00p
○	**Blue Baccy**	Catherine Cookson	£1.25p
○	**Go Tell it to Mrs Golightly**	Catherine Cookson	£1.25p
○	**Matty Doolin**	Catherine Cookson	£1.25p
○	**Mrs Flannagan's Trumpet**	Catherine Cookson	£1.25p
○	**Our John Willie**	Catherine Cookson	£1.25p
○	**The Animals of Farthing Wood**	Colin Dann	£1.75p
○	**The Borribles**	Michael de Larrabeiti	£1.50p
○	**Goodnight Stories**	Meryl Doney	£1.25p
○	**The Vikings**	Mikael Esping	£1.00p
○	**This School is Driving Me Crazy**	Nat Hentoff	£1.25p
○	**Alien Worlds**	Douglas Hill	£1.25p
○	**Day of the Starwind**	Douglas Hill	£1.25p
○	**Deathwing over Veynaa**	Douglas Hill	£1.25p
○	**Galactic Warlord**	Douglas Hill	£1.25p
○	**The Huntsman**	Douglas Hill	£1.25p
○	**Planet of the Warlord**	Douglas Hill	£1.25p
○	**The Young Legionary**	Douglas Hill	£1.25p
○	**Coyote the Trickster**	Douglas Hill and Gail Robinson	95p
○	**Haunted Houseful**	Alfred Hitchcock	£1.10p

○	**A Pistol in Greenyards**	Mollie Hunter	£1.50p
○	**The Stronghold**	Mollie Hunter	£1.25p
○	**Which Witch?**	Eva Ibbotson	£1.25p
○	**Astercote**	Penelope Lively	£1.25p
○	**The Children's Book of Comic Verse**	Christopher Logue	£1.25p
○	**Gangsters, Ghosts and Dragonflies**	Brian Patten	£1.50p
○	**The Cats**	Joan Phipson	£1.25p
○	**The Yearling**	M. K. Rawlings	£1.50p
○	**The Red Pony**	John Steinbeck	£1.25p
○	**The Story Spirts**	A. Williams-Ellis	£1.00p

All these books are available at your local bookshop or newsagent, or can be ordered direct from the publisher. Indicate the number of copies required and fill in the form below 12

....

Name____________________________________
(Block letters please)

Address___________________________________

____

Send to CS Department, Pan Books Ltd,
PO Box 40, Basingstoke, Hants
Please enclose remittance to the value of the cover price plus: 35p for the first book plus 15p per copy for each additional book ordered to a maximum charge of £1.25 to cover postage and packing
Applicable only in the UK

While every effort is made to keep prices low, it is sometimes necessary to increase prices at short notice. Pan Books reserve the right to show on covers and charge new retail prices which may differ from those advertised in the text or elsewhere